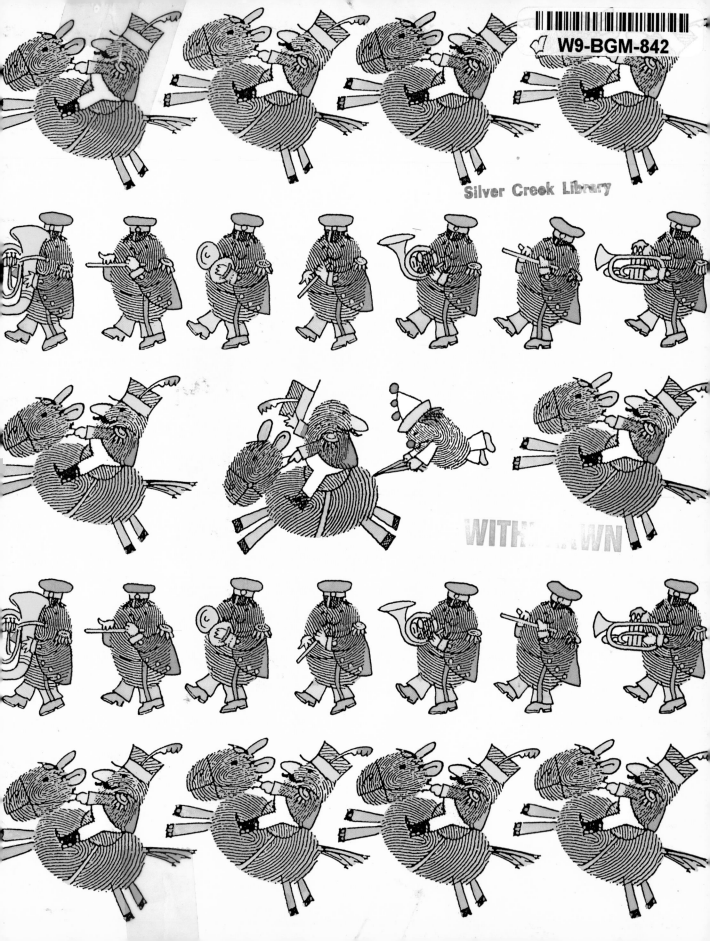

Published by
Delacorte Press
The Bantam Doubleday Dell Publishir
666 Fifth Avenue
New York, New York 10103

This work was originally published in

ISBN: 0-440-50152-0

Library of Congress Catalog Card Number: 88-18101
Manufactured in Hong Kong

First U.S.A. printing
March 1989
10 9 8 7 6 5 4 3 2 1

Rodney Peppé

THUMBPRINT CIRCUS

Delacorte
Press

FOR
NICHOLAS ATTENBOROUGH

Thumbkin was a little clown
who wanted to join the Circus.

"What can you do?"
asked the *Ringmaster*.
"I can help . . . a little," answered Thumbkin.

"Then go and help the *Lion Tamer*,"
said the Ringmaster.
"But don't tread on any tails!"

"Oh, go and help the *Clowns*,"
said the Lion Tamer.
"They need some more water."

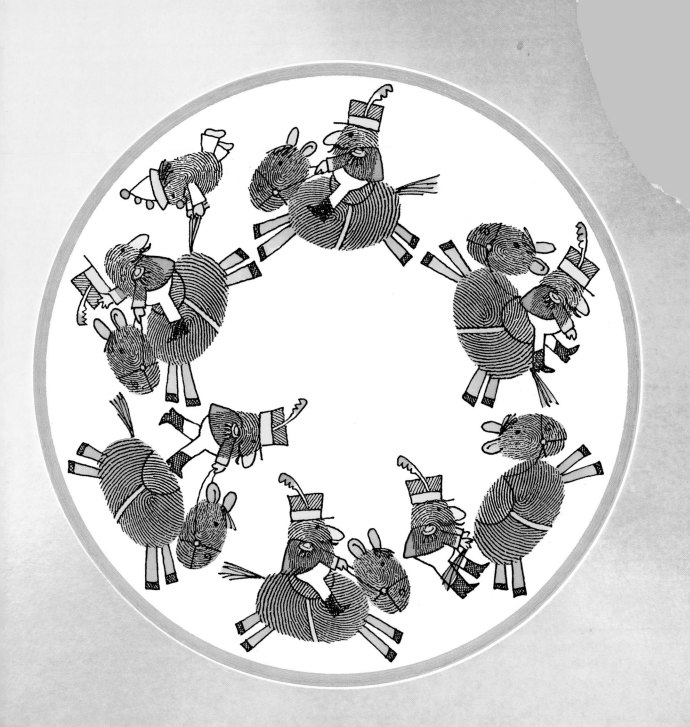

"Now go to the *Trick Riders*,"
said the Clowns.
"They need to slow down!"

"Help the *Trapeze Artistes*,"
said the Trick Riders.
"They need a net."

"Help the *Balancing Bears*,"
said the Trapeze Artistes.
"Their ball's got a puncture."

"Help the *Tightrope Walker*,"
said the Balancing Bears.
"She's going to fall any minute."

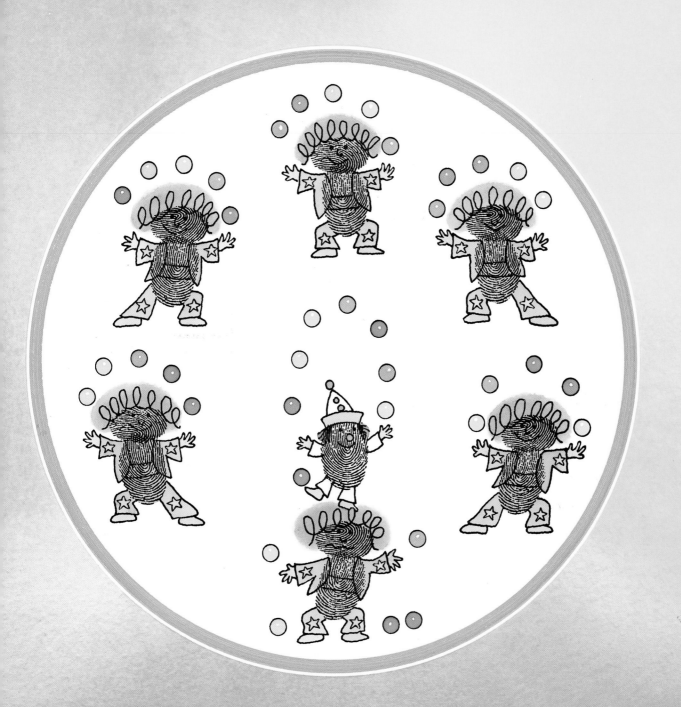

"Help the *Juggler*,"
said the Tightrope Walker.
"He's all butterfingers today!"

The *Acrobats* were leaning over much too far,
but Thumbkin sprang to the rescue!

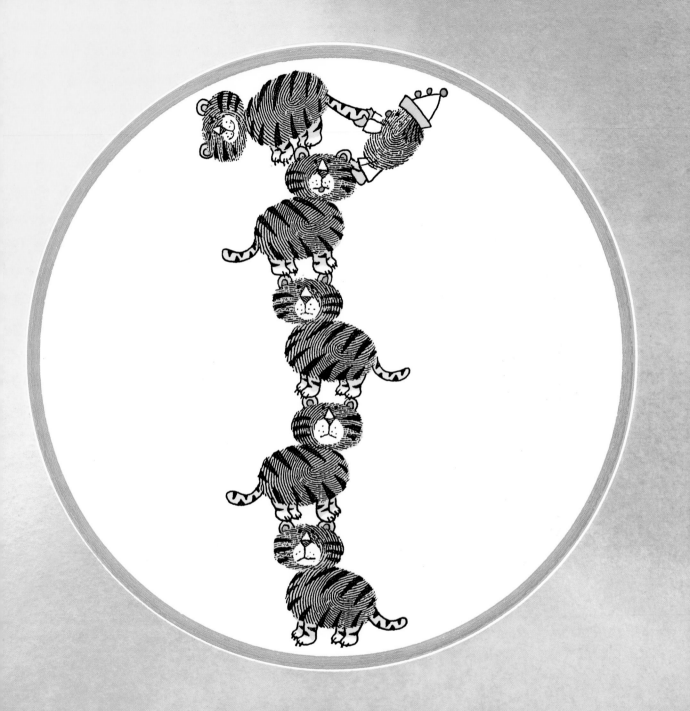

"Now help the *Tigers*," said the Acrobats.
"One seems to have fallen asleep!"

"Go to the *Elephants*,"
said the Tigers.
"The baby needs help with her trick."

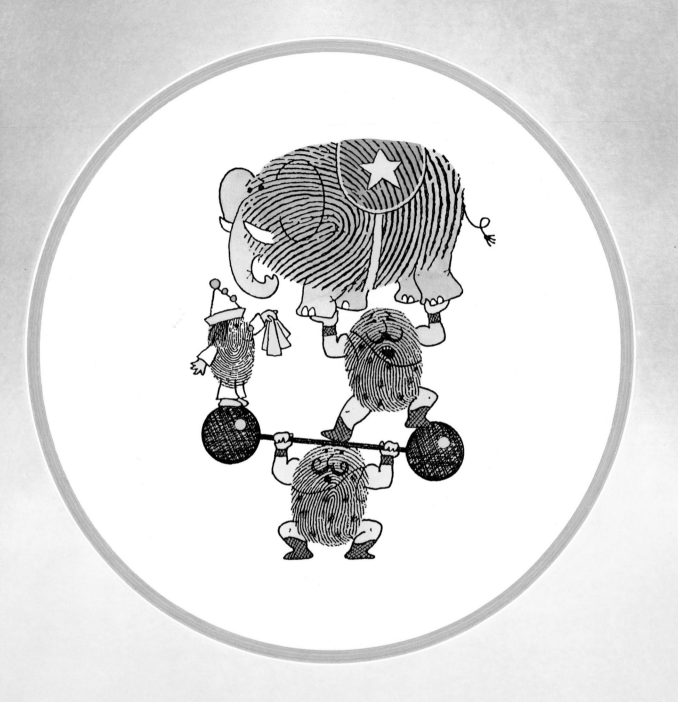

"Help the *Strongman*,"
said the Elephants.
"We think he's about to sneeze!"

"Feed the *Seals*,"
said the Strongman.
"They're getting hungry."

"Help the *Bareback Rider*,"
said the Seals.
"Her horse is tired."

"Help the *Human Cannon-ball*,"
said the Bareback Rider.
"He's not feeling too well just now."

"Where's Thumbkin?" asked the Ringmaster.
"I've lost him!"
answered the Human Cannon-ball.

Everybody looked for Thumbkin.
The audience even looked under their seats.

The *Chimps* stopped their teaparty and looked
under the table. But Thumbkin wasn't there.

"Oompah, oompah, oompah – oomph!"
went the *Bandsman*.
"I've found Thumbkin!" he cried.

The audience cheered *Thumbkin*,
who was the star of the show!

"I like your act," said the Ringmaster
to Thumbkin.
"Do you think you could do it again?"

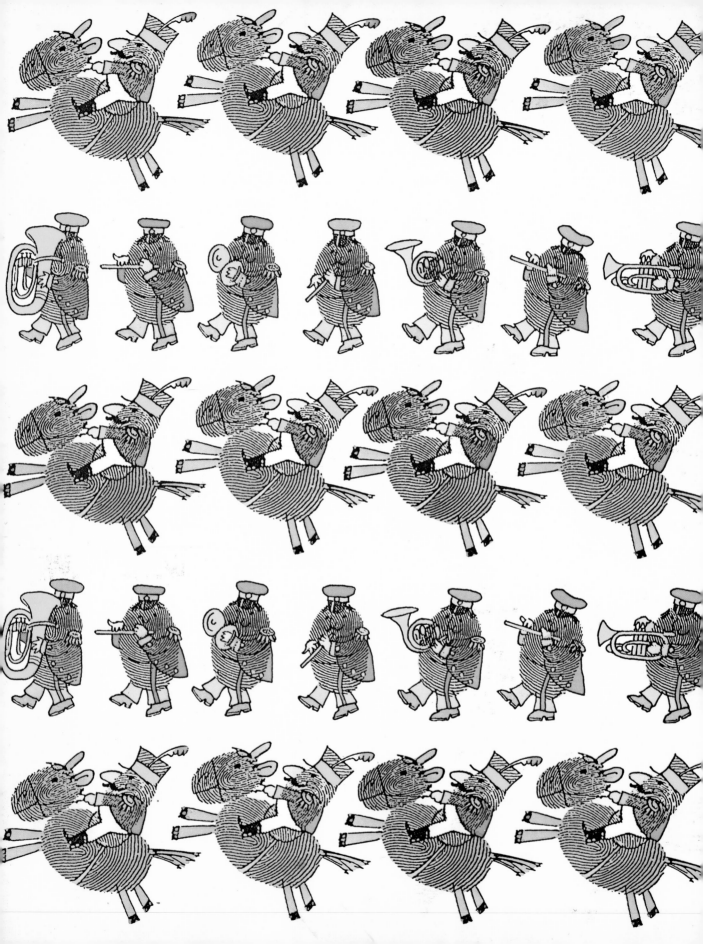